THE PUPPY PRESENT

Collins
RED
Storybook

THE
PUPPY PRESENT
Jean Ure

ILLUSTRATED BY CHRIS CHAPMAN

Collins
An imprint of HarperCollins*Publishers*

This book is dedicated to
the National Canine Defence League –
"A dog is for life, not just for Christmas"

First published in Great Britain by Collins in 1998
Collins is an imprint of HarperCollins*Publishers* Ltd,
77-85 Fulham Palace Road, Hammersmith,
London W6 8JB

The HarperCollins website address is
www.fireandwater.com

7 9 11 10 8 6

Text copyright © Jean Ure 1998
Illustrations copyright © Chris Chapman 1998

The author and illustrator assert their moral rights to be
identified as the author and illustrator of the work.

ISBN 0 00 675152-0

Printed and bound in Great Britain by
Omnia Books Limited, Glasgow

CHAPTER ONE

When Ginger the pup was born, he was one of six. Six little bundles of fur, all warm and wriggling as they burrowed their way towards their mum.

He wasn't known as Ginger then, of course. He was just one of the pups.

To begin with, nobody even knew whether he was a boy or a girl. Then one day someone picked him up, lifted his tail and said, "This one's a boy!"

There were two boys and four girls. They were all honey-coloured except for Ginger, who was – well, ginger! Their mum, who was called Lucy, was half Yorkshire terrier and half

5

something else. No one had ever been able to guess what the something else might be.

As for their dad, he was a great, swaggering, Jack-the-lad who lived up the road and thought no end of himself. He had a bit of red setter in him, so maybe that was where Ginger got his gingerness from.

The puppies all lived together in a big cosy basket with their mum. To begin with, they did nothing very much except sleep and eat. Their eyes were still closed, and they were so tiny they would have fitted into the palm of your hand.

But then, as they grew a little bit bigger and a little bit stronger, they started to explore. One 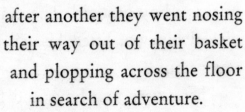 after another they went nosing their way out of their basket and plopping across the floor in search of adventure.

One day Ginger plopped so far t.. lost and couldn't find his way back. He corner, a little blind heap, whimpering f.. mum. But it was all right! His mum knew where he was. He hadn't gone nearly as far as he thought – just across the room, in fact. But it seemed like a really long journey to such a small-sized pup.

His mum pushed him back to his brother and sisters, who all pounced on him, sniffing at him, trying to work out where he had been. Ginger was just glad to be back in his basket! He had given himself a bit of a fright.

When the pups were just over a week old, their eyes opened. They could see! Ginger could see all the way across the room, to the corner where he had sat and whimpered. It still seemed *quite* a long journey.

And now the pups began to play. They played rolling games and tugging games. They played chasing games and chewing games. They scampered and they romped, and every now and again they got a bit rough and had to be told off by their mum. She wouldn't stand for being bitten by a mere scrap of a pup!

Sometimes, a great fluffy thing called *a cat* came to visit them. It got into their basket and sat there, all puffed up and making purring noises while Ginger and his brother and sisters dabbed at its tail and looked in its ears and munched at its fur.

The cat didn't mind. It even rolled over onto its back and let them settle down on top of it. Life was fun for Lucy's puppies!

*

Life wasn't such fun for James Colin.

It *had* been fun, once. That was before his baby brother had come along. Now it was simply horrid!

James Colin had been James Colin right from the very beginning. His mum and dad had chosen his name even before he was born. They had been certain they were going to have a boy, and they did! Just James, all on his own. Which was the way that he liked it.

He had been the most wonderful baby there ever was. He knew this, because his mum and dad had told him so. Lots and lots of times! They had cooed over him and gurgled over him and waggled their fingers into his pram. They had asked him, "Who is Mummy's beautiful boy?" "Who is Daddy's favourite man?" And the answer had always been... James Colin!

For eight whole years he had been 'Mummy's beautiful boy' and 'Daddy's favourite man'. Now a horrible new thing had arrived. It was called Alexander and it was all

red and crumpled and not in
the least bit beautiful.
Sometimes it *smelt*. This
was because it sicked itself
or messed in its nappy.
But Mum still cooed over
it and gurgled, just as she
had with James Colin. Ugh! James didn't know
how she could bear to touch it.

The worst thing was that she expected him
to touch it, as well.

"Come on, James!" she kept saying. "Come
and give your little brother a kiss!"

But James wouldn't. He didn't want a little
brother! He hadn't asked for one. He had been
quite happy being James, all on his own.

"Oh, now, don't be like that!" begged his
mum. "You know we still love you just as
much."

Being loved just as much wasn't enough.
James wanted to be loved *more.* He wanted to
be number one, the same as he had always been.

In any case, he didn't believe that his mum did love him just as much. If she still loved him, then why didn't she take any proper notice of him any more? Why did she spend all her time with the baby? Feeding it, changing it, *slobbering* over it. She obviously loved the baby far more than she loved James.

James ran into the kitchen and pulled open the back door. He was going to do something bad. Something *really* bad.

He stomped down the path and found a big stick. Then he stomped back up again and slashed with the stick at Mum's flowers. That would teach her! Now she would *have* to take notice of him.

CHAPTER TWO

When they were ten weeks old, Ginger and his brother and sisters were turned out of their nice cosy basket. They were taken away from their mum and the big furry cat and put in a pet shop, to be sold.

Poor Lucy was a bit bothered, just at first, wondering where her pups had gone. She ran round the room, looking for them, and couldn't understand why they weren't there. But then she was taken for a good long walk in the park where she met some of her old friends that she hadn't seen for ages, including her boyfriend, the great swaggering Jack-the-lad who was the puppies' dad. They all raced around and chased one another, and did rather a lot of barking, and by the time she got back home Lucy was quite happy to be on her own again, with only the cat for company.

Puppies were *so* exhausting! It was good to be able to curl up nose to tail, just her and the cat in the basket, without six little nipping, yipping, biting, troublesome pups crowding you out.

In any case, the pups were growing up fast. It was time they went to new homes.

*

James Colin was *supposed* to be growing up. Sometimes, just lately, it seemed to his mum that he was becoming more and more childish.

She said, "You're a big boy, now! You're eight years old! Why are you behaving like a baby all over again?"

James couldn't explain to her that there was a part of him that would have liked to be a baby all over again. He had so much looked forward to being eight years old! But now that he *was*, he wasn't enjoying it one little bit. You didn't seem to get much attention when you were eight. When you were a baby you got all the attention in the world. You were cuddled, you were crooned over, you were sung to, you were rocked, you were admired, you were washed and dried and powdered.

None of that happened when you were eight years old.

But he couldn't say all this to his mum. It was just too – well – babyish. You were expected to be a big boy once you got to be eight. Big boys didn't cry. They didn't get kissed better if they hurt themselves. They *certainly* didn't get washed and dried and powdered. Even James squirmed a bit at that.

What big boys did, they slashed at their mum's flowers and broke them. Just to show her!

James's mum was really upset when she found her flowers all battered and bent.

"James!" she said. "Was this you?"

Slowly, watching his mum from under his eyelashes, James nodded.

"How did it happen?"

"Don't know," said James.

"You must know! Were you playing?"

James frowned, as he thought about it. He

scuffed his feet on the grass.

"I won't be angry with you," said his mum, "if you just tell me the truth. Was it an accident?"

James drew a breath. Deep, and quivering. He shook his head.

"You mean, you did it on purpose?"

There was a long silence.

"*Did* you?" said his mum.

"Couldn't help it," mumbled James.

"What do you mean, you couldn't help it?"

"It just happened."

"You mean, you walked into the garden and you thought, 'I'll break down all Mum's lovely flowers'. Is that what you're saying?"

James rubbed a finger over his forehead.

"Well!" His mum looked at him, reproachfully. "That wasn't a very nice thing to do, was it? To break my flowers? It seems to me the sort of thing a four-year-old might do... not an eight-year-old! I would have thought an eight-year-old would have known better. I would have thought an eight-year-old would *enjoy* seeing beautiful flowers."

Eight-year-olds were big boys. They did what they had to do. Breaking flowers was nothing to a big boy!

"I haven't yet heard you say a certain little word," said Mum. She tipped the big boy's face towards her. "Sorry?" she said.

"I couldn't help it!" roared James. "It just happened!"

And he went racing back into the house and up to his bedroom. The bedroom door slammed shut behind him.

His mum was left standing there, with all her broken flowers. The big boy watched her, from behind his bedroom curtain. Why didn't she come upstairs and wallop him? He was a big boy. He could take it!

But his mum just sighed and put the poor broken flowers on the compost heap. Then she went back to the shop, where Dad was serving customers with newspapers and sweets and the baby was being admired in his carry cot.

"I don't know what we're going to do about James," she said.

"Been naughty again, has he?" said Dad.

"I think he's feeling a bit insecure. He thinks we love the baby more than we love him."

"Well, we don't!" said Dad. "We love them both the same. We've told him over and over!"

"Yes, I know." James's mum sighed. "But he asked me the other day if he could have a puppy and I said not until the baby's older. So naturally he blames Alexander."

"It's hardly Alexander's fault," said Dad. "James will have to learn… he can't always have everything just when he wants it."

"He's only little," pleaded James's mum.

"He's big enough! He'll learn. Don't worry, it'll be Christmas soon… his gran will sort him out!"

*

There wasn't anyone to sort the puppies out,

now that they were in the pet shop. No Mum to tell them off, no big furry cat to bop them one if they got a bit too playful. They had to be on their best behaviour if they wanted someone to give them a home!

Ginger had felt a bit anxious, just at first, but not really frightened. Nothing bad had ever happened to him in his short life and he still had his brother and sisters. It was a bit of an adventure!

Even though they were shut up in a cage, life was not boring. There were lots of new sights and sounds in the pet shop. For instance, there was a strange squawking creature, with brightly coloured feathers, that sat on a perch and kept shrieking, "Pretty Polly, pretty Polly!"

Ginger was fascinated. He had never seen anything like it before.

Then there were some funny soft things with long floppy ears and stumpy tails, and some little red-and-gold things that flickered about in a glass case full of water.

And there were people! Lots and lots of people.

Almost all of the people stopped by the cage to look at the puppies. On the very first day, two of Ginger's sisters were sold. On the second day, Ginger's brother was sold.

Ginger really missed his brother. They had been great playmates. The two sisters that were left were rather shy and quiet. They didn't like to bite and pounce and roll about, the way Ginger and his brother had done.

On the third day, a lady came into the shop and said, "I'm looking for a puppy." Ginger's heart leapt. Maybe this would be his turn! His turn to find a person of his own!

The lid of the cage was opened and Ginger jumped up, eagerly.

"Oh, what a sweetheart!" cried the lady. But then her face fell. "Oh dear! It's a boy. I really wanted a girl."

Ginger was put back into the cage and his sisters were taken out. He watched as they squirmed and squiggled. One of them gave the lady a big wet lick on the tip of her nose. The other wagged her tail as hard as she could go.

"I really think I shall have to have both of them," laughed the lady.

And so the puppies were put into a big cardboard carrying box and taken out to the lady's car, and Ginger was left on his own. Nobody to snuggle up to, nobody to play with. Just one small puppy in need of some people.

Ginger crept forlornly into a corner of the cage and lay down with his head between his paws. Why didn't anyone want him?

"There's always one that's hard to get rid of," said the pet shop owner.

Poor Ginger! He didn't realise it, but he was a very odd-looking puppy. He had one ear that stood up and one ear that hung down. His teeth stuck out and his face was all whiskery. He wouldn't have won any prizes in a beauty competition.

"Never mind, little fellow!" The pet shop man waved his fingers at him through the bars of the cage. "Somebody'll take pity on you... sooner or later."

CHAPTER THREE

"Two days to go till Christmas," said the pet shop owner. His eye met Ginger's. It had been a week since the last of Ginger's sisters had been taken away. Ginger had been all alone in his cage ever since.

"Cheer up, little chap!" Even the pet shop owner was beginning to feel sorry for him. "We'll find a home for you."

That very same morning, a lady came into the shop with her little girl. All they had really come in for was to look at the fish.

"Oh, Mum!" The little girl had caught sight of Ginger. "They've got a puppy! Isn't he cute?"

"A bit funny-looking," said her mum.

"Mum, he's not, he's cute! Mum, do you think we could have him? For Christmas? Oh,

Mum, please!" The little girl clutched at her mum's arm. "Please, Mum! He could be my Christmas present!"

"I thought you wanted fish?" said her mum.

"I'd far rather have a puppy! Oh, *please*, Mum!"

"Well... I don't know." The lady looked across at Ginger. Ginger looked back at her. The tip of his tail wagged, hopefully. "It's a mongrel. Who knows what it's going to grow into? It could grow enormous!"

"He won't grow too big," said the pet shop owner. He pointed at Ginger's paws. "Tiny paws, see?"

"Oh, Mum, please! He looks so lonely, all by himself."

The little girl ran across to the cage. Ginger's tail began to fly in circles. He jumped up, with his paws against the netting. Desperately, he scrabbled to get out.

"Mum, he's asking us!" cried the girl. "He's asking as plain as can be! He wants us

to take him."

Ginger renewed his efforts. All the time that he was jumping, he was making little crying sounds.

"He's begging us, Mum! We can't just leave him here. Not at Christmas. Oh, Mum! Say we can have him! *Please!*"

And so the lady gave in. She bought Ginger as a Christmas present for her little girl, because the little girl wanted him so badly, and Ginger himself had asked so nicely.

As for Ginger, he was the proudest puppy

on earth. At last! He had found some people of his own!

"What shall we call him?" asked the little girl. Her name was Maisie. Maisie O'Reilly.

"Red?" said her mum.

"Red's not a name! Red's a colour."

"Rufus?"

"No." Maisie shook her head. She didn't like Rufus.

"How about... Ginger?"

"Ginger. Yes! We'll call him Ginger." Maisie dropped a kiss on top of Ginger's head. "Ginger O'Reilly," she said. "Our Christmas puppy."

Ginger wasn't to know that Christmas comes but once a year. He wasn't to know that sometimes a dog is *only* for Christmas. He thought that love went on for ever.

There was lots of love, to begin with. All over Christmas, Ginger was one of the family.

He was given little bits of turkey to eat, and he joined in all the games. He helped pull the crackers, and Maisie took a paper hat and cut two ear holes in it and stuck it on his head.

Everyone laughed as Ginger ran round the room in his paper hat.

Ginger liked it when they laughed; it meant they were pleased with him. He started to show off and snatch crackers out of the box and shake them. Then he ran at the tree and grabbed a magic lantern.

"Stop him, stop him, for heaven's sake!" cried Maisie's mum. "He'll have the whole thing down!"

"Let's give him his present," said Maisie, and she held out a package wrapped in red tissue paper. "Here you are, Ginge! This is for you!"

Ginger took the package away to a quiet corner. It smelt good! He held it between his front paws and tore at the paper with his teeth.

"Clever boy!" Maisie clapped her hands. "He's unwrapping it!"

Inside the tissue paper was a big, bone-shaped biscuit. Ginger's Christmas present! He lay down immediately to eat it.

"You mind you clear up that mess after him," said Maisie's mum.

"Oh, Mum! It's Christmas!" wailed Maisie.

"I don't care. I'm not having all those crumbs trodden into the carpet."

No one was cross with Ginger, because he was only a puppy and didn't know any better.

"It's your fault for giving it to him in the sitting room," said Maisie's mum. "He should have had it in the kitchen."

On Boxing Day an aunt and uncle came to visit with their two children. Maisie and the children played chasing games with Ginger all up and down the stairs and in and out of the bedrooms. The children cried "Hoo, hoo!" and ran at Ginger with their arms held above their

heads. Ginger streamed
down the stairs and
into the kitchen and
back up the stairs and
underneath a wardrobe
and over a bed and
back down the stairs,
wild-eyed and panting.

In the end he grew
so over-excited that he made a little puddle on
the hall carpet.

"That's the trouble with dogs," said Maisie's
aunt. "They make the place filthy."

"He's only a baby," said Maisie. "He isn't
house-trained yet."

"Rub his nose in it and chuck him in the
garden," said Maisie's uncle. "It's the only way
he'll learn."

But Maisie had heard a vet on television say
that you should never punish a puppy for
making a puddle in the wrong place. You
should take him into the garden and praise him

and pat him when he made one in the *right* place.

"It was my fault," said Maisie. "I should have taken him out."

"You're too soft," said her uncle. "He needs a good walloping."

"I'm not walloping Ginger!" said Maisie.

After all, you didn't wallop a baby for doing a puddle in its nappy; why should you wallop a puppy?

"It's up to you to teach him," said Maisie's mum.

Maisie promised that she would.

CHAPTER FOUR

James Colin had a Christmas tree all covered in spangles and sparkles and ropes of tinsel. It was *his* Christmas tree. His very own. Nothing to do with the baby. The baby was too young for Christmas trees. All the baby could do was wave its fingers and go "Gaaah!"

At the foot of the tree were great piles of presents. They were the small presents, that were opened after breakfast. Some were for the baby, but most were for James. The baby didn't understand about Christmas. It was just a waste of money, buying presents for it, but everyone did. Even James had had to buy it a cuddly toy. He hadn't wanted to, but his mum had insisted.

"He's your brother! Of course you must buy him a present. He'll buy one for you!"

His mum was telling fibs. The baby couldn't buy James a present. It didn't have any money, for one thing; and for another, it couldn't walk or talk, so how could it possibly go out and buy anything? It couldn't! All the same, there was a present that said 'To James with love from Alexander'. And when he opened it his mum would say: "Now give Alex a kiss and say thank you."

She was always trying to make James kiss it. But James wouldn't! He wasn't *ever* going to. He liked to pretend that the baby didn't exist.

On Christmas Eve, Gran arrived. James ran to let her in.

"How's my best boy?" cried Gran. And she gave James a big hug and a kiss.

James's heart swelled with pride. *He* was

Gran's best boy! Not everyone was interested in silly smelly babies.

"Come and see my tree!" He tugged at Gran's arm. "Come and see all my presents."

"My, what a rush we're in!" Gran stood in the hall, unbuttoning her coat. "Give an old lady time to get her breath! Where's the new arrival? Where's my second-best boy?"

"You don't want to see him." James said it anxiously. "He's very boring. He does nothing but sleep."

"Oh, what a wonderful quiet baby he must be!"

"Sleep and yell," said James, quickly. "Sometimes he sleeps and sometimes he yells. As a matter of fact," said James, "he yells more than he sleeps. He does a *lot* of yelling. Really loud sort of yelling. He yells most of the time. Just yells and yells for no reason."

"There's always a reason," said Gran. "Poor little mite!"

"He's not poor." A note of desperation

entered James's voice. "He's really bad-tempered. He bashes things with his rattle. I don't think you'd like him."

"Nonsense!" said Gran. "Get away with you!" She gave James a little push. "I liked you when you were a baby, didn't I?"

That was different, thought James. James had been a *beautiful* baby. He opened his mouth to say so, but Gran was already leading the way down the hall.

"Come on!" she said. "Let's go and take a look at him."

In the end, Gran was just as bad as everyone else. Coo coo, gurgle gurgle.

"Who's his granny's little sweetheart, then?"

It made James *sick*.

But even James couldn't go on feeling sick all over Christmas. Especially not on Christmas morning, when he woke to find a pillow case stuffed full of presents at the end of his bed! These were his *big* presents. His important presents.

He dragged the pillow case with him into Mum and Dad's room and hauled it up onto their bed. Dad groaned and tried to go back to sleep again, but of course he couldn't. It was far too exciting!

"Let's see what you've got," said Mum.

James dipped his hand into the pillow case and pulled out the first present.

"Wow!" said Dad. "What's in there?"

James tore at the wrapping paper. A book? A football annual! Brilliant! He dived back into the pillow case. Very soon, the bed was awash with a sea of brightly coloured wrapping paper and streams of red ribbon.

"What's this?" said James, pulling the last parcel out of the pillow case.

Mum smiled. "That's the dog you wanted."

"*Dog*?" said James.

For a moment he actually thought it might be a real dog that Mum had tied up in Christmas paper and put into the pillow case. But of course you couldn't do that with a real dog; it would be cruel. And of course it *wasn't* a real dog. It was a pretend dog. A computer dog.

"You have to look after it just as you would a real one." His mum said it eagerly. She did so want James to be happy with his dog! "You have to feed it and groom it and play with it."

"And give it a name," said Dad. "What shall we call it? Rover?"

James put the pretend dog back in its box.

"I'll think about it," he said.

"That's right!" Mum nodded, approvingly. "You can't give a dog just any old name. You have to get to know it first."

How could you get to know a *computer* dog? You couldn't take it for walks. You couldn't stroke it or pat it. You couldn't cuddle it in bed.

James knew his mum was trying her best to please him, but he almost wished she hadn't given him the computer dog. He wanted a real dog! He could have had one if it hadn't been for the baby.

"When you're eight years old," his mum had always said.

And now here he was, almost eight and a half, and all he got was a pretend dog! Because of the baby.

The baby was too young. If they had a real dog, the baby might hurt it. Or the dog might hurt the baby.

And anyway, a dog would take too much looking after. Mum already had her hands full helping Dad in the shop. The shop was downstairs, at the front. It sold sweets and groceries and newspapers. It was always very busy. Mum didn't have time for a dog *and* a baby.

So why couldn't they have had the dog and

not the baby?

James rubbed his eyes and swallowed a lump that had suddenly appeared in his throat. This was Christmas Day! You couldn't cry on Christmas Day. After all, he had known he wasn't going to have a dog. He'd been trying very hard not to think about it. Now this – this *computer* thing had gone and brought it all back.

"Let's go and make a cup of tea," said Mum, "then you can take one in to your gran."

It was good snuggling under the duvet with Gran while she drank her tea. James took some of his presents in to show her.

"My! You *are* a lucky boy," said Gran. "And I hear you've got a new puppy, too?"

James frowned. "It's not a real one."

"No, well, people shouldn't give real puppies as presents," said Gran. "'Specially not at Christmas."

"Why not?" said James.

"Because sometimes, once Christmas is over, people get bored with their new puppies. They think they're just a nuisance and they can't be bothered with them any more."

"I wouldn't be like that," said James. He plucked at the corner of Gran's duvet. "They had some puppies in the pet shop. Mum wouldn't let me have one."

"Quite right!" Gran nodded. "Puppies should not be sold in pet shops. A pet shop is no place for a puppy. They should be kept with their mothers, and people should go and see them in their own homes."

James pleated the duvet through his fingers.

"They had this big notice in the window, PUPPIES FOR SALE. Mum wouldn't even let me go and look at them!"

"I expect she didn't want you to be tempted."

"But she *said* I could have one when I was eight years old!" James threw the duvet away from him. "It's all the baby's fault."

There was a pause.

"The baby didn't ask to be born,"

murmured Gran. "I don't think it's very fair to blame him. Do you? Honestly?"

James pursed his lips.

"He's so tiny and helpless," said Gran. "And you're so big and strong! Alexander needs taking care of just the same as a little puppy would."

"That's Mum's job!" roared James. He would take care of a puppy, if only Mum would let him have one. Mum could take care of the baby.

"It's all she ever does!" James scrambled off the bed. "Takes care of it!" He swept up his presents and made for the door. "All day long, all she ever does!"

CHAPTER FIVE

Christmas was over, but Ginger's people still loved him. Well, Maisie still loved him. She took him into the garden after every meal and said, "Good boy, Ginge! Be a good boy!" And if he was a good boy she praised him and patted him, and Ginger's tail flew in circles. He almost burst with pride when Maisie was pleased with him.

Sometimes he wasn't such a good boy and then Maisie looked grave and said, "*Bad* boy, Ginger! *Dirty* boy!" and Ginger drooped and tucked his tail

between his legs and was shut out all by himself in the garden. But never for very long. Maisie couldn't bear to be cross with him! It always ended up with a kiss and a cuddle and a whispered 'Sorry' from Maisie because she'd called him a dirty boy.

Life was good for Ginger. He was too small to go for walks, but Maisie threw a ball for him in the back garden and taught him 'Fetch' and 'Sit'. At night he slept in Maisie's room on a special dog blanket, and Maisie's mum fed him dishes of delicious food and thought it really funny when he started tugging at the fringes on the rug or burying doggie biscuits under the back-door mat.

Only Maisie's dad had any doubts. He wasn't unkind to Ginger but he didn't ever pet him or cuddle him like Maisie and her mum did.

"It's all very well for now," said Maisie's dad, "but what's going to happen when the novelty wears off?"

Maisie thought her dad was a real old grump.

What did he mean, 'when the novelty wore off'? The novelty wasn't going to wear off!

She swept Ginger into her arms.

"He's my very own puppy and I shall love him for ever!"

But then there came a day when everything changed for Ginger. His little life began to fall apart. Maisie went back to school, her mum and dad went back to work, and suddenly Ginger was on his own, shut away in the kitchen with a bowl of water and a dish of dog biscuits and told to 'Be a good boy'.

Ginger couldn't understand it. 'Be a good boy' meant going into the garden with Maisie, being praised and patted. Not shut away all by himself in the kitchen!

Never in his life had Ginger been on his own. Not completely on his own. There had always been someone. His mum, his brother and sisters, the man in the pet shop. Even when his sisters had gone and the pet shop had been shut up for the night there had been the squawking creature and the furry things. Now there wasn't anyone.

The first time it happened he was really frightened. Why had they left him? Had he done something wrong? Was he being punished? Were they ever going to come back?

In a frenzy, Ginger began biting and scratching at the bottom of the door. He had to get out, he had to get out! If he could only get out, he might be able to find them.

But the door was firmly shut, and wouldn't open. And in his panic Ginger had overturned his water bowl and all the water had gone streaming across the floor.

Ginger pointed his nose at the ceiling and began to howl. He howled and he howled, as if his heart were breaking. His people had gone and he would never see them again!

After a while, he sank down with his nose pressed to the door crack, his ears alert for any sound that might just mean they were coming back.

But they didn't.

Outside it grew dark, and Ginger was still on his own. He whimpered and scraped again at the door. He was thirsty, but there wasn't any water left. The dog biscuits were still there, but he felt too anxious to eat.

Before they had gone, Maisie's mum had spread newspaper on the floor. He didn't know why she had done that. He leapt on it and tore it fiercely into shreds. Bits of newspaper flew everywhere.

For a moment he felt better. He sat back, his tongue lolling. The newspaper had obviously been put there for him to do something with. Well, he *had* done something with it! He had torn it up. They would praise him and say what a good dog he had been.

If they came back.

And then at last, when he had almost given up

hope, he heard the sound of a key being turned. He heard footsteps along the passage and the voices of Maisie and her mum. Joyfully, Ginger sprang to his feet. The kitchen door opened and Maisie appeared, looking very smart in her school uniform. Ginger hurled himself at her, barking, his tail flying in circles.

"Careful!" screamed Maisie. "Watch my tights! Oh, Ginger, *stop* it! You'll make holes in them!"

Maisie's mum came into the kitchen. She saw the shredded newspaper and the overturned water bowl. Then she saw the bottom of the door, where Ginger had bitten and scraped in his desperate attempts to get out.

"Oh, you naughty dog! she cried. "You bad, naughty, *wicked* dog!"

And she gave him three sharp whacks across the nose.

Ginger cowered. What had he done? What had he done that was wrong?

"Don't you ever, *ever*—" Maisie's mum

grabbed him by the scruff of his neck and dragged him across to the door. "Ever, *ever* do such a thing again!"

Maisie tried her best to speak up for him.

"He couldn't help it, Mum! He didn't know it was wrong."

"Well," said her mum, "he'd better learn, that's all I can say." She tightened her lips into a thin straight line. "I'm not having a dog that wrecks the place. He either learns or he goes."

*

Ginger wasn't the only one who was in trouble. James Colin was, too.

"James Colin," said his mum, "you have been a very naughty boy! What is the meaning of this?"

She pointed sternly at a big round hole that had appeared in the carpet in James's bedroom. James shuffled his feet.

"You deliberately cut a hole!" said his mum. James did not deny it.

"Why? What on earth did you do it for?"

James hunched a shoulder. "Felt like it."

"What are you talking about? You *felt* like it?"

"Felt like cutting a hole."

There was a moment of silence. James could tell that his mum was really cross. He could tell that she would really have liked to slap him, only that was something she never did.

He wouldn't have minded. She could slap him if she wanted. At least if she was slapping him it meant that she was paying attention to James rather than the baby.

That was why he had cut the hole. Because he had known that it would make her mad and that she would come and ask him questions about it. She would want to know what he had done it for. She would have to spend *time* with him.

"I don't know." His mum shook her head. "I just don't know what to do with you. You used to be such a good, sensible boy. I really used to feel that I could depend on you. Now—"

Now? James waited, eagerly. Now what? What was she going to say about him?

Nothing!

From the other room, the baby started crying.

"There's the baby," said Mum. "I'll speak to you later, young man!"

Mum turned and left the room. The baby had only to open his mouth for Mum to go running. James could cut a huge great hole in the middle of his carpet and she couldn't even spare him five minutes.

What did he have to do to get her attention?

CHAPTER SIX

Poor Ginger! His life was going from bad to worse. He had been a Christmas puppy; and now that it was no longer Christmas it seemed that no one loved him any more.

Every day he was left on his own, shut in the kitchen for hour after hour. Every day when his people came back it seemed that he had done something wrong. Either he had chewed something or spilt something or made a puddle where he shouldn't.

He didn't jump up, now, when the people came in. He had learnt that they didn't like that. They pushed him away, quite roughly, and screamed at him to 'Get down!'

He didn't even sleep in Maisie's room any more. One night he had had a little accident on the carpet and Maisie's mum had said, "We can't have this! The kitchen is the place for dogs."

So now he not only spent all day in the kitchen but all night, as well.

He was old enough to go for walks, but nobody bothered to take him. Maisie's mum said that Maisie ought to do it – "He's your dog! You were the one who wanted him" – but Maisie never seemed to have the time. In the morning she was always in a rush for school, and in the evening it was too dark, or she had homework, or there was something she wanted to watch on television.

"He's got the garden," she said.

But even in the garden Ginger did things wrong. He dug holes where he shouldn't have dug holes and pulled things up that he shouldn't have pulled up. And then he got hit or shouted at and told he was a 'Stupid dog' until in the end he was almost too scared to do anything at all.

"I told you the novelty would wear off," said Maisie's dad. "We ought to find a new home for him."

But Maisie didn't want that. Ginger was her dog and she loved him – when she remembered. Sometimes even now she would throw a ball for him or pick him up and kiss him. Ginger's heart almost burst with happiness when she did that. Unfortunately, she didn't do it very often. In fact she did it less and less. Ginger's tail hardly ever wagged, these days.

And then half term arrived at Maisie's school, and Maisie and her mum and dad went off to visit Maisie's nan and grandad.

"What shall we do with the dog?" said Dad. "We can't take it with us."

Nan and Grandad didn't care for dogs.

"It's all right, said Mum. "We can leave it in the garden. It's not going to starve in that short time. It's only three days, we'll be back Sunday night."

"But suppose it rains?" said Maisie.

"He can go in the shed," said Mum.

So Ginger was left in the garden, with a bowl of water and a dish of dry dog food. He was tied with a length of rope so that he couldn't reach the flower beds and dig holes, or tear up the flowers. Maisie was going to go and kiss him goodbye but at the last moment she forgot.

"Oh!" she said, as Dad started the car. "I didn't say goodbye to Ginger!"

"You're not going back now," said Dad.

"But, Dad, he'll wonder where we've gone!"

"Maisie," said Mum, "it's only a *dog*."

Ginger may have been only a dog, but he could still feel sad, and lonely, and confused. He could also feel bored.

He ate up all his food in the first few minutes. What to do next? Every time he tried to go anywhere, the length of rope yanked him back. Right! He would have to get rid of the rope.

Ginger lay down and started chewing.

He chewed and he chewed, and by the middle of the morning he had chewed the rope in two.

By the middle of the afternoon, he had dug an enormous hole in one of the flower beds. He knew they would beat him for it, and yell at him, but it was just such fun! Ginger, after all, was still only a puppy. He couldn't always control himself. And he had lots and lots of energy! If he wasn't taken for walks, he had to find some other way of using it up.

The hole that he dug went right underneath

the fence and out the other side. Ginger didn't know what lived on the other side, but the more he thought about it the more he was tempted to find out.

He made up his mind: he would go exploring!

He didn't rush things. He had never been out in the world before; he wasn't sure what to expect. His small whiskery face, covered in ginger fur, peered out cautiously from under the fence. He saw pavement, and grass, and trees. It looked inviting! Ginger wriggled his way through.

Once outside he stood for a moment, sniffing the air, then turned and went trotting up the road. Every now and again he would stop to investigate an interesting smell, and once or twice he passed other dogs, on leads.

The other dogs had people with them. The people seemed a bit concerned that Ginger was out on his own. One of them tried speaking to him. He said, "Good boy! Come on, then!" and clicked his fingers, but Ginger wasn't sure of people any more. It seemed safer to keep away from them. You never knew when they were going to cuff you or give you a kick. Ginger took to his heels, and ran.

Ginger discovered that there were good things in the outside world, and bad things, too. These were some of the good things:

An overturned dustbin, spilling out scraps of food. Ginger nosed about for a long time by the dustbin. Dustbins were definitely good.

A cat sitting on a wall, sunning itself. Ginger still had faint memories of a cat from some time in his past. A big furry one that had purred and let Ginger curl up with him. Cats were good! He liked cats.

A big red ball, lying in the gutter. Ginger pounced on it, with glee. A toy! He knew about toys. He had had some, once, before Maisie's mum had thrown them away. (She said they were dirty, which was because Ginger had tried burying them in the garden.)

The red ball was also quite dirty, but it made a lovely loud squeaky noise when Ginger bit into it. He played with the ball for some time, until in the end it rolled away from him, into the road, where a car squashed it flat.

Cars were one of the bad things. Ginger was scared of cars. He'd never seen any before and it frightened him the way they roared and belched and rushed along at such a pace. It frightened him even more now that he knew they could squash things flat.

Another bad thing was a big fierce dog that he met in a doorway. The dog took one look at Ginger and hurled itself at him, snarling and frothing, its lips pulled back over long yellow teeth. It was twice the size of Ginger. It could have snapped him in two with just one bite.

Ginger screamed with terror and rolled over

onto his back. From somewhere a man's voice yelled, "Sable! *Leave!*"

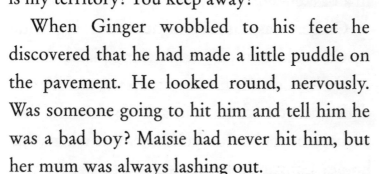

Sable backed off, but not before he had taken a quick snap. Ginger knew what the snap meant: "This is my territory! You keep away!"

When Ginger wobbled to his feet he discovered that he had made a little puddle on the pavement. He looked round, nervously. Was someone going to hit him and tell him he was a bad boy? Maisie had never hit him, but her mum was always lashing out.

Ginger was scared of Maisie's mum. It hadn't been so bad when Maisie was there to protect him, but Maisie didn't seem to care about Ginger any more. She didn't care if her mum shook him or kicked him or hurled him into the garden. He had just become a nuisance.

Ginger put his tail between his legs and crept away. Away from the puddle and the big fierce dog. He hadn't known there were dogs that attacked other dogs. It made him feel very small and insecure. He couldn't trust people, he couldn't trust dogs. Even the cat on the wall had spat at him when he had jumped up to say hello. Not like the lovely furry one that he remembered from the days when he had lived in a basket.

Ginger was discovering that the big wide world could be a very frightening place.

He kept on the move until in the end it grew dark and started to rain, and he thought that perhaps he had better go home. But where was home? Ginger no longer knew. He was lost!

Some boys were coming towards him, shouting and laughing and kicking tin cans. One of them saw Ginger and called out to him.

"Doggie, doggie! Come here, doggie!"

Ginger cowered and slunk away. The boy held out a hand.

"Here, doggie! Nice doggie! Want some food, doggie?"

Ginger hesitated. The boy was offering him something. Something that smelt good. It smelt like… chocolate! Ginger remembered chocolate. Maisie had given him a tiny square at Christmas, as a 'special treat'. He licked his lips. It seemed a long time since he had found the overturned dustbin and nosed out some food.

Ginger crept forward, low to the ground, his ears flattened and his tail wagging hopefully. The boy held out the chocolate. As Ginger went to take it, a hail of tin cans came smashing into him. Bish! Bosh! Bash!

The boys guffawed. They thought it really funny.

"Har har har!" went the boys.

One of them swooped on a bottle and booted it, very hard, straight at Ginger. The one that had held out the chocolate aimed a kick at Ginger's head. The others set up a chant.

"Get the dog, get the dog, get the dog!"

Ginger turned and ran, as fast as his wobbly puppy legs would carry him. The boys galloped behind, whooping and shouting.

"Get the dog, get the dog!"

Ginger's heart pounded in his rib cage. He had never been so scared in all his life. Another tin can caught him on the shoulder.

"Get the dog, get the dog!"

Maddened with fear, Ginger dashed out into the road. A car jammed on its brakes and pulled up with a screech only centimetres away from him. The driver leant out of his window and bellowed, angrily.

"Get that dog off the road!"

"It ain't ours," said one of the boys. And they went on their way, rather quickly, before they could be accused of causing an accident.

The driver hooted furiously on his horn. In panic, Ginger bolted – straight down the road, into the path of a large container truck. There was a *thub*, as Ginger and one of the nearside front wheels came into contact.

Ginger grunted. His body went hurtling through space. The truck drove on. The driver, sitting high up in his cab, had no idea that he had almost run over a small ginger puppy.

After a while, the breath came back into Ginger's body. Slowly and painfully, he picked himself up and went limping off into the shadows, dragging one leg behind him. He was cold, he was wet, he was exhausted. He was also very, very frightened.

Poor Ginger! He hadn't known that such terrors existed. He thought of Maisie, who had called him her very own Christmas puppy. Where was Maisie now? Why didn't she come and help him?

Maisie couldn't. She was miles away, at her

nan's. She had no idea that her Christmas puppy had escaped into the big wide world and almost been killed. In any case, she was enjoying herself! She had forgotten all about her Christmas pup.

Whimpering, Ginger dragged his poor battered body under a hedge and curled himself into a ball. What else could he do? Even if he had known how to find his way home, his people weren't there. They had gone away and left him.

Ginger could be dead for all they cared.

CHAPTER SEVEN

James Colin was running away from home. He had made up his mind. Nobody loved him any more. All they cared about was the baby. Dad had said to him at breakfast, "I'm warning you, my boy! I'm not going to tolerate much more of this sort of behaviour."

James had said, "*What* sort of behaviour?" and brought his spoon down with a satisfying *plap* into his cereal bowl so that a great shower of milk and Rice Krispies had gone splatting across the table. Some had landed on the baby. Hah!

Dad had roared, "*That* sort of behaviour!" and leant over to give James a sharp smack on the hand.

Mum hadn't stuck up for him. She hadn't told Dad that it was an accident and that you shouldn't ever punish your children by hitting them. All she had said was, "Oh, James, *really*! Now look what you've done!" And she had gone jumping up to see to the baby.

Fuss fuss fuss! Just because a tiny weeny little drop of milk had landed on it.

"Your manners are getting worse and worse," scolded Mum.

"Manners?" said Dad. "What manners? He hasn't got any manners! He's becoming a thoroughly rude and unpleasant little boy and I'm not sure that I like him any more."

"Neither do I, when he behaves like that," said Mum; and she wiped the baby's face, very tenderly, with a piece of kitchen towel and went, "There, there! All nice and clean again."

As if the baby cared! It was always messing

itself up. The baby *liked* being dirty.

Now it was nine o'clock and Dad was in the shop, serving customers. Mum was in the storeroom, sorting boxes. It was then that James decided: he was going to run away. He would run as far and as fast as he could and they would never see him again. Then they would be sorry!

He took a plastic carrier bag from one of the kitchen cupboards and began filling it with food. He put in an apple and an orange and a banana. He put in a packet of biscuits and a packet of crisps and a bottle of Coca-Cola in case he got thirsty. He reckoned that should be enough to keep him going.

Then he opened the kitchen door and crept out, very quietly, so that Mum wouldn't hear him and come running to fetch him back. He had a sort of feeling that probably, in the end, he *would* come back, but not until they had appeared on television and begged him.

In his imagination he saw his mum, with tears streaming down her face, and his dad, very pale, standing beside her.

"Please, James! Wherever you are... come back to us! We want you, we love you! We didn't mean to be unkind to you!"

But that wouldn't happen until he had been gone for about... six hours. At the very least! They had to have enough time to start getting worried and to be sorry for the way they had treated him. If Mum caught him now she would just get mad at him for helping himself to food. And for going into the road, which he wasn't meant to do.

James ran down the garden path and unbolted the back gate. The back gate led into a grassy passage with garages at one end, where James's dad and his neighbours kept their cars. James thought about going to sit in the garage and get started on some of his food, but he managed to resist the temptation. It wasn't time to start eating just yet. He was running away!

He ran as far as the end of the passage. And there he stopped. Something had caught his eye. Something under the hedge. What was it? It looked like a bit of old fur coat – except that old fur coats didn't whimper. This one was definitely whimpering.

James set down his carrier bag. He knelt, cautiously, to take a closer look. From under the hedge a pair of eyes peered up at him. It wasn't a fur coat. It was… a dog!

The next minute James was racing back up the passage, up the garden path, in through the back door, across the kitchen, out into the hall, shouting as he went: "Mum! Mum! Come quickly! I've found something!"

James's mum came hurtling out of the storeroom. For once she even left the baby behind.

"What's the matter? What is it? What are you shouting about?"

"I've found something, Mum! I think it's hurt!"

Together, Mum and James went running down the garden path.

"Out here!" said James.

"Out here?" said Mum. "What were you doing out—"

"Look!" cried James. "Under the hedge!"

"*Oh*!" Mum was down on her knees in an instant. "It's a puppy! Oh, the poor little thing! It's absolutely drenched… run, James, and fetch a blanket! Quickly! A blanket or a big towel. Anything will do. Just be quick!"

James snatched the first thing that he could find. It was a blanket from the baby's pram, but Mum didn't even seem to notice.

"We must get him to the vet," she said. "Immediately. Go and tell your dad while I get the car out!"

James ran into the shop. In front of all the

customers he shouted, "Dad, I've found a puppy and we're taking him to the vet!"

"You're what?" said his dad.

"Taking him to the vet!" shouted James.

"What for?" said his dad; but James had already gone hurtling back into the house.

Mum had taken the baby out with her to the car, but she had left the puppy wrapped in its blanket on the kitchen floor. James squatted down and very gently stroked it.

"Puppy," he said. "Poor puppy!"

The puppy cringed, as if it thought James was going to hit it.

"It's all right, puppy!" James spoke crooningly, as he had heard Mum do with the baby. "I'll take care of you!"

Mum had come back.

"I'll need you with us, James. I'll need you to keep an eye on the baby."

James really didn't see why the baby couldn't have been left in the shop with Dad. Did it always have to go *everywhere* with them? He grumbled about it to his mum. "Why can't we leave the baby with Dad?"

"Oh, James! Don't be difficult," said Mum. "You know Dad's busy serving customers."

Carefully, Mum picked up the puppy and carried it out to the car. She told James to get into the back with the baby and to hold the puppy next to him.

"Gently! Don't hurt him."

James sat there, with the puppy on one side of him and the baby on the other. He tried showing the puppy to the baby, but the baby just lay there in its special baby seat, kicking its legs and making the 'Gaa gaa gaa' noise that it made when it was happy. It probably thought they were going out in the car just for fun.

"Sick doggie," said James. You had to talk to babies in baby talk or they didn't understand. "Sick doggie, going to vet."

"Gaa," said the baby, blowing a few bubbles.

James gave up. It didn't even seem to understand baby talk!

There was an old lady with a cat in the vet's waiting room, but she took one look at the puppy and said that Mum had better go in first.

"That's very kind of you," said Mum.

"Quite all right," said the old lady. "Felix is only here for his teeth. Your little dog looks very poorly."

"He's not ours," explained Mum. "James found him under a hedge. We think the poor little thing must have been in some kind of an accident."

"The vet will make him better," said James, "won't he? Won't he, Mum? He'll make him better?"

"I'm sure he'll do his very best," said Mum. "You stay here and look after the baby for me. Can you do that?"

James made a grunting noise. He supposed he could, if he really had to. He would far rather *not* have had to. He still didn't see why it couldn't have been left in the shop with Dad. It could have been put on the counter in its carry cot and all the customers could have come and 'oohed' and 'aahed' at it.

"I know I can trust you," said Mum.

Mum and the puppy went into the surgery. James was left on his own, holding the baby. He felt a bit nervous. He had never held the baby before. Suppose he dropped it? It might break, like Mum's flowers!

The old lady leant over to look.

"Is that your little sister?" she said.

"Brother," said James. He felt a bit indignant. How could anyone mistake Alexander for a girl? He didn't look in the least like a girl!

"How nice that your mum can trust you to look after him," said the lady. "You must be a very mature and sensible young man. And what a lovely baby!"

James looked down at the baby. Was it lovely? The baby suddenly broke into a big smile. James was so surprised that he went and smiled back before he could stop himself.

"He obviously loves you," said the lady.

James nodded, rather sternly. Just so long as it didn't do anything in its nappy before Mum came back. Just so long as it wasn't sick, or anything.

The baby behaved itself really well. James was quite proud of it. He supposed, on the whole, it wasn't a bad sort of baby as babies went. Not as good as a puppy, of course!

It seemed ages before Mum came back, but at last the surgery door opened and there she was with the puppy still wrapped in its blanket.

"Is he going to be all right?" said James.

"Yes!" Mum smiled. She was obviously just as relieved as James. "The vet says he's very badly bruised and shocked, but nothing's broken. He'll pull through."

James felt like jumping up and punching the

air, only he couldn't because of the baby. He squeezed the baby very tightly, instead.

"Can we keep him, Mum?"

"Well… no. I don't think we can do that," said Mum. "After all, he's not ours, is he?"

"But I found him!" said James.

"Yes, I know you did, and I'm sure his owners will be extremely grateful to you. I shall tell them that you were the one who rescued him. But it still doesn't make him ours. He's such an adorable little chap! Someone, somewhere, is bound to be looking for him. They're certain to want him back."

James chewed rather hard on his bottom lip.

"How will they know where he is?"

"They'll ring the police to report that their puppy is missing and the police will tell them."

"How will the police know?"

"The police will know because I'm going to call them just as soon as we get home."

"So where will he be?" said James.

"At the police station!"

James crinkled his brow. "Locked up? In a cell?"

"In a special dog cell."

Mum went over to the desk to pay the vet's bill, while James sat and thought about what she had said. He imagined the puppy locked up in his cell. Police cells were horrid! Grey and cold and bare, with stone floors and iron bars on the door. No soft blankets to snuggle into. After all, they were meant for criminals.

Poor puppy! He wasn't a criminal.

"Why can't we keep him until his owners come?" said James.

"I don't think we could do that," said Mum.

"Why couldn't we?" said James.

"Well, because… we don't know how long it would be! It could be days. Who would look after him?"

"I would look after him," said James.

"You?" said Mum.

"I could! I could look after him!"

"He certainly seems like a very mature and

sensible young man," said the cat lady.

Mum looked at James.

"*Are* you a mature and sensible young man?"

"I've held the baby!" said James.

"So you have," said Mum. "You've held him very nicely. All right! We'll take the puppy home and you can look after him. He's your responsibility!"

CHAPTER EIGHT

"So this is it, is it?" said Dad. The shop had closed for the day and Dad had come through to the house for his tea. "This is the puppy?"

He looked at the small ginger heap lying on the hearth rug. A pair of anxious brown eyes looked back up at him. Slowly, not quite certainly, a tail gave a little wag.

"He's saying hello to you!" said James.

"And how long is he going to be here?" said Dad.

"I told James," said Mum, "that we're only looking after him until his owners get in touch."

"*I'm* looking after him," said James.

"James is looking after him," said Mum. "Because he's a good sensible boy and he held the baby for me."

"And because I'm mature," said James.

"And because he's mature," said Mum.

"I'm very glad to hear it." Dad squatted down, to take a closer look at the puppy. "So we don't know anything about the little chap? No name or address tag?"

"Nothing," said Mum. "People are so irresponsible! But I've rung the police and given them the details."

"What shall we call him?" James had knelt down, with Dad, beside the puppy. "He ought to have a name!"

"Well, but I expect he's already got one," said Mum. "I don't think we should give him another. It might confuse him."

"And remember," said Dad, "he's only going to be here for a short time. His owners could turn up any moment."

"He's got to have a name." James said it stubbornly. "I'm going to call him Ginger, 'cos that's what he is."

The puppy didn't seem in the least confused by being called Ginger. He thumped his tail and wriggled, as if he were used to it.

James lay down on the rug and put his arm round Ginger's neck. "See, he's licking me!"

"Just don't get too attached to him," warned Dad. "I'm not at all sure," he added to James's mum, "that this was a good idea."

Ginger would have disagreed. Ginger couldn't remember when he had last felt so secure and so loved. The little boy had spent all day stroking him and whispering to him.

"Poor puppy! It's all right now, puppy! You're safe now. I'll look after you."

Sunday came, and no one telephoned to say

that they were Ginger's owner. Mum said that James could take Ginger into the garden and play with him, just for a short time.

"But be gentle with him! Remember, he's been very badly bruised."

James and Ginger had a gentle game of ball and then went for a gentle stroll round the garden.

"These are the flower beds," said James. "We're not supposed to play on those in case we break Mum's flowers. This is the lawn." He patted at the grass. "We can play on the lawn. We can play anywhere, really, except the flower beds. This is my tree that I climb. This is the garden shed. This is the bird table. And this," said James, "is the compost heap."

Ginger really liked the compost heap. He jumped on it and rolled on it and covered himself all over in delicious smells.

"For goodness' sake!" said Mum, when James and Ginger came back indoors. "What *has* that dog been up to?"

Ginger immediately cringed. He thought James's mum was going to beat him. He was so frightened that he made a little puddle on the kitchen floor.

"Mum! What's the matter with him?" cried James.

"He's terrified," said Mum, "that's what's the matter with him." And she knelt down and held out her hand and told Ginger that it was all right, she wasn't cross with him. "I'm not going to hit you!"

"Mum never hits anyone," said James. "Not even me," he added.

"Yes, and there are times when James deserves it," said Mum. "But not you, little chap!" She picked Ginger up and kissed him. "You haven't done anything naughty."

Ginger could hardly believe it. He had been out in the garden, he had walked on the grass, he had rolled in the lovely smelly heap, he had made a puddle on the floor – and no one had smacked him for it!

"Can I show him the baby?" said James. "He'd like to see the baby."

Ginger had never met a baby before. He and the baby looked at each other. Ginger sniffed, cautiously. The baby gurgled and waved its starfish fingers.

"Nice doggy," said James. "Nice baby!"

Next thing he knew, Ginger's little pink tongue had gone snaking out and planted a wet doggy kiss on the baby's hand.

James held his breath. Now what would the baby do?

The baby kicked up its legs and crowed with delight.

"He likes him!" said James. "The baby likes him!"

"That's good," said Mum. "Maybe when Alex is a bit older—"

"He likes *Ginger*!" roared James.

"Now, James!" His mum wagged a finger at him. "You know what we agreed... just until his owners come."

But maybe his owners never would? James crossed his fingers. Please, *please*, don't let Ginger's owners come!

Sunday was almost over. James had had his bedtime bath and been allowed back downstairs for a final cuddle with Ginger. He sat on the sofa with Ginger beside him. If Ginger had dared to get on the sofa at his other home, there would have been trouble. He would have been yanked off by the scruff of his neck and thrown squealing to the floor. But here, nobody seemed to mind. Nobody ever got cross with him, or shouted. Ginger hated it when people shouted. It usually meant that a kick or a blow would be coming his way.

He closed his eyes and gave a great sigh of contentment as he snuggled down next to James.

"I think he's settled here, Mum," said James. "Don't you?"

And then, at eight o'clock...

"Telephone!" said Mum.

"I'll get it."

Dad left the room. He came back looking rather grave.

"James, I want you to be a big brave boy," he said. "That was Ginger's owners. They've been away for the weekend and they've just got back. They're coming round to fetch him."

James's lower lip began to tremble.

"We did warn you," said Dad.

A tear went plopping down James's face.

"Darling, think of Ginger," urged Mum. "They're his people. He'll be so happy to see them!"

But Ginger wasn't happy. He wasn't happy at all. When the door opened and Maisie and her mum came in, he shrank close to James as if for protection.

"Ginger!" cried Maisie; but Ginger flattened his ears and wouldn't go to her.

"That wretched animal!" said Maisie's mum.

Ginger shivered. "Chewed through his rope and dug a hole right under the fence, if you please! Now I suppose we owe you a small fortune in vet's fees."

There was a pause.

"You're not telling me," said Mum, "that you went away and left him tied up all weekend?"

"Well, we couldn't take him with us." Maisie's mum sounded quite aggressive about it. "My mother-in-law won't have dogs in the house. He'd have been nothing but a nuisance. To be perfectly honest, we should never have got a dog in the first place. It was Maisie talked me into it. Goodness knows why! She never takes the thing out or exercises it."

"I will, Mum! I promise!"

"That's what you said before. We'd be far better off getting rid of it."

"No!" Maisie stormed across the room. "He's my dog! I want him!"

She snatched at Ginger by his ruff. Ginger

gave a terrified yelp.

"You stop that!" James rushed forward. "You stop doing that! You'll hurt him!"

"He's my dog," said Maisie. "I'll do what I like."

"But you're hurting him! You're frightening him!" James was almost sobbing. "Mum! Stop her!"

Mum and Dad exchanged a quick glance. Then Mum stepped forward. Very firmly, she removed Ginger from Maisie's grasp.

"I'm sorry," she said, "but I really don't think that anyone who goes away and leaves a young puppy tied up in a garden is fit to keep a dog. Do you?"

Maisie opened her mouth, but her mum got in first.

"If that's the way you feel," said Maisie's mum, "then I suggest you keep him. Come along, Maisie."

"But, *Mum*—"

"I said, come along," said her mum. "We'll

get you something else, instead. A new pair of trainers, or something."

"I'll see you out," said Dad.

When Dad came back, Ginger was curled up on James's lap, on the sofa.

"Well! It looks as if we've got ourselves a dog after all," said Mum.

"Can he be mine?" said James. "Just mine and nobody else's? 'Cos I was the one who found him. And I'm grown up. I can look after him. The baby can't. He's too young. Isn't he, Mum? The baby's too young!"

"Far too young," agreed Mum.

"I'm mature," said James.

"You are. I think you've proved that."

"However," said Dad, "mature or not, it's way past your bedtime."

"Ginger's, too," said Mum.

"Go on," said Dad. "Off you go!"

James stood up, holding Ginger in his arms.

"Can Ginger sleep with me?"

Mum and Dad spoke at the same time.

Mum said, "Yes, I suppose so, if you want."

Dad said, "Certainly not!"

James beamed.

"Thanks, Mum!"

Dad threw up his hands.

"Why do I bother?"

"You let the baby sleep with you," said James. "And that's all Ginger is... just a baby."

"Oh, get on with you!" said Dad. "It doesn't seem to matter what I say, I'm always overruled."

But he was only pretending to be cross. Even Ginger knew that.

"Go on, then," said Mum. "I'll come and tuck you both up."

As Mum was leaving the bedroom, she suddenly stopped.

"By the way," she said, "you never told me what you were doing, when you found Ginger. What did you go out of the garden for?"

"I was running away," said James.

"Good heavens!" said Mum. "Were things as bad as that?"

"Yes, but they're all right now," said James. "Because I've got Ginger."

James had Ginger and Ginger had James. And they were just as blissfully happy as a boy and his dog could be.

Rainbow ANIMAL HOSPITAL
Steve Attridge

Sick pets and injured animals –
every day brings a new emergency for Eddie
and the staff at the Rainbow Animal Hospital.

Thumper the Brave

Eddie is both hopping mad and grief-stricken when
he is told that Old Cheesy, the chief vet, has found
a new owner for Thumper, Eddie's special pet at the
hospital. He didn't even give Eddie the chance to
say goodbye. Eddie is determined to visit Thumper
and discovers his new owner is going to use him
in a toothpaste commercial for television…

If you care about animals and
love adventure stories,

is for you.

Collins

ST. TIGGYWINKLES WILDLIFE HOSPITAL

Jaws the Hedgehog and other stories by Les Stocker

St. Tiggywinkles Wildlife Hospital started out as a shed for injured hedgehogs - it is now the leading wildlife hospital in Britain and Eruope's first wildlife teaching hospital.

Find out which baby animal eats what at St. Tiggywinkles and join in the drama of real-life rescues. Meet Jaws - the hedgehog who learnt to bite back; Eric - the deer with a temper; Bisto - the badger with a sore head and P. C. Wildcat - the tiger in pussycat clothing!

Six endearing stories from everyday life at the world's most famous wildlife hospital, written by its founder and director.

Collins

THE
ENCHANTED HORSE
by Magdalen Nabb

The magical story of Irina, a little girl who finds a
dusty wooden horse in a junk shop. Irina's mother
and father have little time for her, even though it is
Christmas, so Irina spends all her time loving and
caring for the little horse made of wood – until one
night, the horse stamps its hooves and whisks
Irina away on an enchanted gallop through the night.
This is the first of many secret rides, but when the
enchanted horse hears the hooves of the wild horses,
she gallops away from Irina who fears she'll never see
her beloved horse again. But the horse does come
back, and leaves Irina a very special present.

Children's Choice for the Smarties Award

Order Form

To order direct from the publishers, just make a list of the titles you want and fill in the form below:

Name ....

Address ....

....

....

Send to: Dept 6, HarperCollins Publishers Ltd, Westerhill Road, Bishopbriggs, Glasgow G64 2QT.

Please enclose a cheque or postal order to the value of the cover price, plus:

UK & BFPO: Add £1.00 for the first book, and 25p per copy for each additional book ordered.

Overseas and Eire: Add £2.95 service charge. Books will be sent by surface mail but quotes for airmail despatch will be given on request.

A 24-hour telephone ordering service is available to holders of Visa, MasterCard, Amex or Switch cards on 0141- 772 2281.

Collins
An *Imprint* of HarperCollins*Publishers*